TO RALPH, FOR ALWAYS INSPIRING ME
& TONY, FOR CONSTANTLY ENCOURAGING ME.
XXX

ISBN: 978-1-9997628-8-9

First published in the UK
August 2019 by Owlet Press
www.owletpress.com

THE BROWNEST MOUSE IN TOWN

BY TARAH .L. GEAR

ILLUSTRATED BY CHRISTINE CUDDIHY

The Polka Dot Pet Shop
that's just down the street,
has colourful creatures
you'll be dying to meet!

There are heaps of hamsters
with bright, rainbow fur,
running ever so fast,
their feet start to blur.

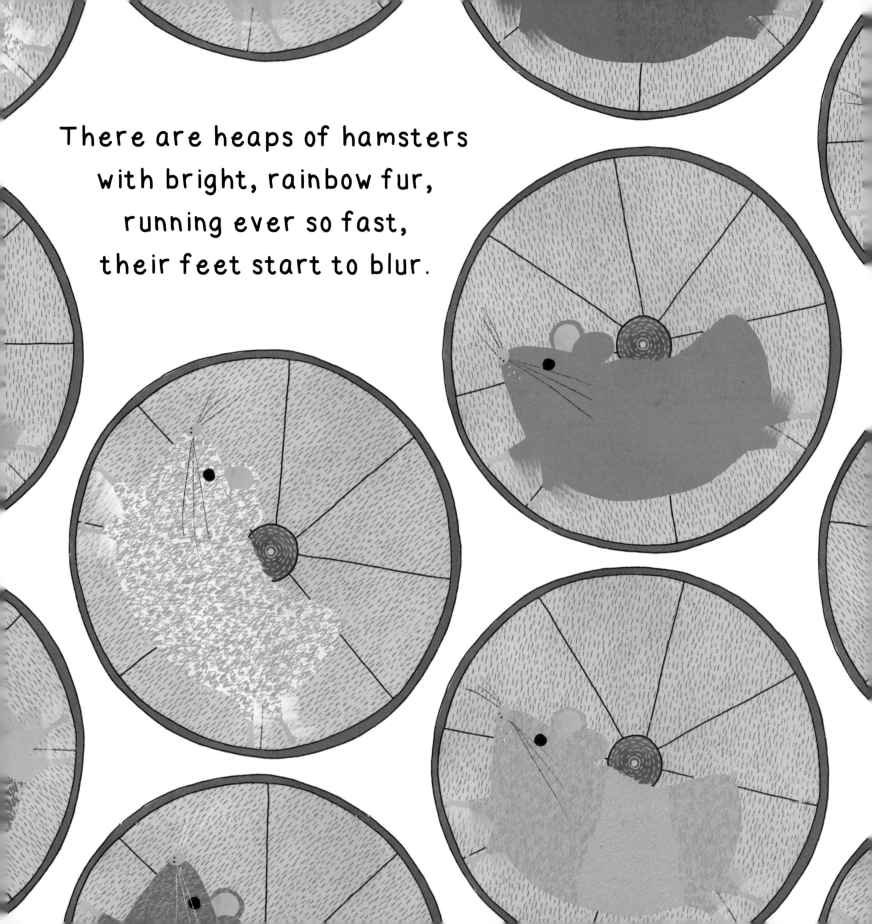

The lizards are laced
with big frilly collars,
while the guinea pigs
look like a million dollars.

Even the gerbils
have long flashing tails,
while under the counter,
sit glow-at-night snails!

Then there's one little mouse, who longs to fit in,
but he doesn't have patterns or colourful skin.

He doesn't wear glitter or have shiny hair,
like the disco chinchillas. Oh my, what a pair!

He hopes and he dreams
of a desperate wish,
to be covered in stars,
like the tropical fish.

"I know I'm just brown,"
the mouse sadly sniffed;
but (between you and me)
<u>this</u> mouse had a gift.

He thought of a plan,
this mouse who could talk.
He whizzed round his cage
in search of some chalk.

The very next day,
people queued for the mouse,
who'd chalked the words 'show time'
on the front of his house.

He then climbed the ladder,
to the top of his cage,
gently clearing his throat
before 'taking the stage'.

"I'm only a mouse,
a mouse that's just brown..."

"...but everyone knows,
I'm the BROWNEST MOUSE IN TOWN!"

News travelled fast.
Crowds would gather each week,
to see the brown mouse,
watch him write and hear him speak.

He didn't need glitter
or rainbows because
he knew he was special.
They could all see he was.

OWLET PRESS

Growing into wisdom

Discover more stories to treasure!

Sol has the craziest dinner time when he finds elephants in his custard! This playful story promotes positive mental health in younger children, by helping them to talk about their feelings and utilise support from family.

RRP: £6.99

All the weasels in Westburrow Wood like to be the same, but not Wesley; he's obsessed with clothes! This story of acceptance helps children build empathy, by exploring themes around differences and identity.

RRP: £7.99

Well, maybe just a little peek? Discover worlds of wizards, super heroes riding dinosaurs and magical forest creatures to name a few. This book excites reluctant readers and inspires avid readers to write creatively.

RRP: £6.99

Follow @owletpress on social media or visit www.owletpress.com to learn more about us.